NAKED POEMS

by

Barry Blackwell
M.A., M.D., M.Phil., FRCPsych.

Buy Mine!

Authors who write books feel
the need to scratch an itch.
Readers can decline.

For Richard
Fellow Poet
from
Barry

To order additional copies of this book, contact:
Xlibris
1-888-795-4274
www.Xlibris.com
Orders@Xlibris.com
750576

DEDICATION

This volume is dedicated to the residents and staff of Saint John's, an ecumenical Episcopalian retirement community. These citizens comprise a vibrant, sharing and caring, socially engaged assembly of elderly folks who dwell by the shoreline of Lake Michigan. Much credit ascribes to *Kathie Eilers* who, during her Presidency, displayed the wisdom and leadership to craft an innovative culture of *Almost Home* as well as helping plan and shepherd to completion an architecturally impressive South Tower, twin to the home-like North Tower.

TABLE OF CONTENTS

PREFACE

Poems are not for everybody. In my 35-year familiarity with the genre I have found great pleasure and intellectual enjoyment in exploring different poetic forms to help explain the way in which intellect and emotion interact to influence what appears on the page and how that may color the reader's response. Words, like clothes, both conceal and reveal what lies beneath the surface. I employ this metaphor of making a poem naked to readers by presenting the same topic in four different forms and examining the result. This approach to enjoying poems is what I wish to share.

An op-ed in the Sunday New York Times some years ago, by William Logan, a distinguished poet, was titled, *Poetry, Who needs it?* Logan also authored a book with an even more provocative title, *Guilty Knowledge, Guilty Pleasure, The Dirty Art of Poetry.* His succinct thought-provoking views include, "The dirty secret of poetry is that it is loved by some, loathed by many, and bought by almost no one."

I count myself among the minority precisely because of this interest in looking closely at the different sources, forms, and content of poems. As a psychiatrist, I can speculate how others may feel puzzled, confused, or irritated by unusual semantics and varied structural forms or disturbed by thinly disguised raw emotion which T.S. Elliot described as "private experience at its greatest intensity." My hypothesis is that enhancing interest in the intellectual and structural aspects of a poem may magnify, mitigate, or mold emotional responses to it.

Logan also notes that poetry has been "long ago shoved aside in schools . . . when it is taught at all, it's too often as a shudder of self-expression . . . another way to bully them into feeling compassion or tolerance." In short, poetry is too intimate, too revelatory, too embarrassing to enjoy. Why inflict it on others?

9

On the credit side Logan points to "the difficulties and majesties and the subtleties of meaning that make poetry . . . poetry is what language alone can do." This is what captivated me from the beginning, when, 35 years ago, I enrolled in a summer writing course at UWM taught by our local poet Jim Hazard. I was quickly entranced by the tension and interplay between the creative and the expository, the emotion and the intellect, the left and right brain linked by a bridge, the corpus callosum that integrates all our feelings with thoughts. Themes emerge from deep within, from the unconscious, intuition, empathy and emotion. But their literary expression on the page is crafted to some degree by the intellect and conscious mind in form, rhyme, assonance, metaphor, meter, analogy, alliteration and humor. This is an orchestration of interacting thoughts and feelings that entertains and informs.

In a slim 2016 volume, *The Hatred of Poetry,* Ben Lerner confesses, "Poetry and the hatred of poetry for me, and maybe for you, are inextricable." Lerner attributes this to the fact that poetry arises from a desire to go beyond the "finite and historical" to reach the "transcendental and divine." He continues, "But as soon as you move from the impulse to the actual poem the song of the infinite is compromised by the finitude of its terms." Mere word content, form, and structure fail to convey the transcendent and divine. Of course this is an interpretation that applies to a small genre of poems with masterpiece intentions above and beyond the mundane majority, like mine, that aim merely to inform, entertain or tickle the senses. That said, it is the bold contention of this impertinent amateur and very minor poet that dissecting a poem, even in that narrow corridor, is an intrepid attempt to convert hatred to understanding, appreciation, or fondness. A review of Lerner's book (*NY Times* 8.28.16) notes that surveys of American reading habits suggest that the audience for poetry has shrunk by two-thirds since 1992. To judge the success or failure of this slim volume in reversing that trend lies with the reader.

A PREPARATORY PROJECT

To set the stage for the remainder of this book and the poems it analyzes and discusses, I decided to challenge myself in a way that might better illustrate the process by exploring the metaphor behind the title *Naked Poems*. In this case likening words in poetry to clothes in couture: the ways in which both conceal and reveal what lies naked beneath the surface.

What follows is the metaphor expressed in four different forms: a Haiku doublet, a sonnet, a classical form and rhyme scheme, and a free-form poem. You are invited to examine and assess the form itself as well as the content and structure within each. To what extent does each form capture the spirit of the metaphor? Which do you think achieves its goal the best? What elements in the structure contribute to the success and your enjoyment of the poem? Does this process enhance, enlighten, distress, distract, or spoil your enjoyment of each poem?

Haiku Doublet

Metaphor I

Poems are couture,
As words shape thoughts and feelings,
Clothes mold form and flesh.

Metaphor II

To enjoy them more
I must implore you, do please
Perform a strip tease!

The Haiku and Senryu are Japanese rhyme schemes dating from the 17th century consisting of only three lines of 5, 7, and

5 syllables. Despite their brevity they can be remarkably flexible. Haiku were about nature, serious, and had to include a *kigo*, or seasonal word. Senryu were humorous, satirical and often about human foibles. As the form spread to other cultures these distinctions have become blurred and Haiku is used, as here, generically, although most of mine are technically Senryu.

Sonnet

Unmasked

Adorned in lavish vestments, just designed
Which tempt a roving eye, the seeking kind.
Silken velvet, to which the rich aspire,
Garments that flaunt and stir repressed desire,
Rainbow pigments, in shades inclined to shock,
An audience, pretending not to look.
Can I describe, in common words, the urge
Such displays arouse, yet need be purged
Lest coarse manners inflame the public eye,
Make some ashamed and others justly shy?
While her seamstress toils to hide the naked flesh
The mistress seems immune to that distress.
      But poets must unmask hypocrisy
      Amidst a carnal aristocracy.

The sonnet (little song) originated in Italy in the 13th Century. It has 14 lines, each with 10 syllables, where alternate syllables are stressed giving it a lilting rhythm known as iambic pentameter. The last word of alternate lines rhyme and the last two lines are a rhyming couplet, set back from the margins, to provide a concluding emphasis. Shakespeare wrote 154 sonnets, mostly to lovers, female and male, with themes of romance and mortality.

Free Form

Cover Up

We are
Earth's only creatures
For whom nature's surface
Does not suffice,
Whose camouflage
Invites, incites or satisfies.

Clothes
Shield us from shame,
Mask our modesty.
Layers from chill,
Skimp for humidity.
Glimpses to arouse,
Textures that tingle.
Custom made or
Couture a la mode.

Concealed
Beneath clothes,
Like meaning
Under words.
When stripped of those,
Only then is
Naked truth
Exposed.

There is very little structure, form, or classical content in *Cover Up*. There are a few subtle ones—can you detect them?

A Classic Form

Disrobed

Both clothes and words
Cause deception,
Trick the senses,
Wake perceptions.

Garments conceal
Faults forbidden,
Blemish and flesh
Best kept hidden.

Designs incite
Carnal glimpses.
Kindling desire,
Stir impulses.

Poems portray
Hidden meanings.
Bold metaphors,
Buried feelings.

Stanzas that rhyme
Assist the mind,
Making meaning
Easy to find.

Free form poems
Use obscure words
Parse strange ideas
Some find weird.

This classical poem, *Disrobed,* has 6 stanzas of four lines each and every line has four syllables. The second and last lines rhyme. There are, of course, many different variations in classic form and structure possible.

INTROSPECTION

Where does a poem and its content come from and why does it adopt a particular form?

We can approach this question from either side of the conundrum. In the Preparatory Project I took the content, a metaphor, and expressed it in four different but common forms, each of which we analyzed. For the remainder of the book, using poems I have written that fall under particular subject headings, I hope to illustrate the relationships that exist between the form and the content of each poem.

Introspection is first because it gets to the heart of where poems come from. Is it a preoccupation with current events, thoughts, or feelings, or do they arise from a deeper, preconscious level of concern? I will examine five poems from a psychological perspective, each one in a different form.

This question usually remains unanswered, the origin undisclosed, perhaps because to reveal might be akin to spoiling a joke by explaining it. Or the poet prefers a reader to discover truth hidden beneath words. This can be tricky or embarrassing. Literary critics often seek to explain a writer's work in biographical terms, also a dangerous enterprise since it seeks to diminish or replace creativity with explanations derived merely from the author's perceived character or life experiences. I shall unveil the poems and invite you to test the truth against your imagination as well as the impact of understanding on your enjoyment and your assessment of creativity. Does revelation enhance or detract? Would you sooner know or not know where the poem came from?

Pale as the Sheet that Shrouds Her

Disease has smudged the mirror
of her too familiar face.

Perched in a sterile dome,
audience to a white ballet,
I view the butchery and eavesdrop
while they pluck her womb
and snip it from her tangled gut.
My crimson origins glisten
In a stainless dish.

Apprentice, I learn the trickery.
A deft mechanic ties the bleeders,
debates the baseball scores,
teases the scrub nurses, chides the residents,
teaches the students. Left and right brain
doing different chores. In sleep when
the halves embrace, the surgeon dreams.

It doesn't work for me. Dreamless,
awake, I watch and weep.

Afterwards, in Recovery, she bleeds;
first a trickle, then a deluge.
Loitering outside her cubicle
an intern hands me a warm tube.
If the lab can find some absent factor
her blood may clot and stop. But
I arrive too late. A weary technician,
eager for home, won't cooperate.

Rage contracts in me, pushing memory
deep into dreamtime.

Pale as the Sheet that Shrouds Her declares itself readily. I am
watching a surgeon operate on my mother, part detached observer,

part deeply disturbed, both by the surgery and its probable but unspoken fatal outcome in which I play a frustrating role. The poem's structure is unusual. There are three descriptive stanzas of increasing length that lead towards the climax, but they are interspersed with terse declarative doublets that convey emotion. The content also reveals the role of dreams for both the surgeon and the witness in integrating affect with intellect: technique and teaching for the surgeon, rage and memory for the observer. Within the structure, impact is achieved by imagery rather than word play. There are only a few incidental rhymes (late, co-operate; clot, stop) and some alliterations (first stanza) with teases... scrub; teaches... students; watch and weep, deft, debates, doing, different, dreams. Only the last two stanzas are an actual memory, everything else is a product of my imagination.

In middle age my mother underwent a hysterectomy and several years later developed intestinal adhesions leading to bowel obstruction. At the time, in 1962, she was 56 years old and I was a 28 year old newly qualified house officer to one of Britain's leading surgeons at Guy's Hospital in London. My distressed father phoned to explain the situation, the surgeon agreed to operate and I signed off the case. My mother died without regaining consciousness from delirium tremens, due to alcoholism that I knew about but never revealed before the operation.

Fourteen years later, in 1976, aged 42, I became Chair of Psychiatry at a brand new medical school at Wright State University in Dayton. The Dean, a surgeon, asked me to give an introductory lecture to the incoming students on *Being a Doctor* (published as *Dream Doctor* in the Archives of Internal Medicine, April, 1984). Anxious about the task a few days before the address, I had a dream.

I was treating a woman newly admitted to the hospital with a bleeding disorder. I decided to set up an infusion but was uncertain of what drug to use. The ward copy of the "Physicians' Desk Reference" *was missing so I was forced to make a fruitless search elsewhere. Returning to the patient's bedside I found the intern had started an infusion. As I approached the bed the patient began to bleed profusely around the infusion needle. The flow of blood grew rapidly from a trickle to a deluge. I grabbed at the sheets in a futile attempt to staunch the bleeding as I became aware of the beseeching eyes of the intern, the recriminatory eyes of the nurse, and the terrified eyes of the patient. Then I awoke.*

The dream encapsulates the unique stresses of a physician's role: the necessity to make immediate decisions in ambiguous situations, to take control in emergencies, to be responsible for finding a cure. Understanding these imperatives is essential to the process of training medical students. Attempts to teach empathy and "behavioral medicine" principles compete poorly with lifesaving interventions in an overcrowded curriculum. So I decided to use the dream in my talk, presenting it as a real case.

After the talk my Vice Chairman, a psychoanalyst, asked who the real woman was. Only then did I remember my mother. This is one of the very few poems in my collection for which no date is recorded, nor can I recall when it was written.

Happily Ever After

Widowed solitude spread in her
like a virus breeding resistance.
She sold the cows, the fields, the farmhouse,
down to their antique silver spoons.
Beggared, persuaded by the culture,
She bought five years of boarding school.
As the train shuffled out, she shouted,
"Be good, I love you dearly son."
Bereft, feeling alone, he doubted that.

Her sacrifice minted tougher coin
in all male routines, incessant bells,
cruel classrooms, muddy football fields.
Calloused, his ambition seeded
inside a carapace. He left equipped
to climb the twisted vine of business.
There was plain terror on the way up
plotting takeovers, forcing mergers,
toppling corporate giants. He reached the summit.

Past forty he paused. Eligible, unwed,
her provider and protector,
only hers. A fairy tale come true.
Safe at last, united with a man,
Expressing joy not felt before,
She flung her arms around his neck
but sensed the reflex pulling back
and looking deep into his face
she softly said, "Don't you love me Jack?"

The content of *Happily Ever After* is fairly clear although there are nuances that only those familiar with boarding school life might note. A widowed single parent decides to sacrifice her possessions and perhaps status in order to send her only son to boarding school around puberty, hoping this will ensure his success in life at the same time that she stifles her own emotional solitude. But the son's success comes with a price: unease with the open expression of emotion, a side effect of incarceration in an all-male, highly competitive environment.

The structure of the poem is hybrid. It has three 9-line stanzas, with varying syllables and no rhyme scheme although there is sporadic word play, a few alliterations (provider, protector) and occasional rhymes (shouted, doubted; climb, vine; neck, back, Jack). Each stanza has a metaphor, a virus breeding resistance, the twisted vine of business and a fairy tale. The prevailing affect is sadness, contrasting the business success of the son with the loneliness of the mother.

The content of the poem has deep roots in my own experience of boarding school. In 1938 at age four my mother and father took me to India when my father became the sales manager of a large tea company. They left my brother, aged eleven, behind in boarding school and, after the Second World War, which began a year later, he did not see his mother for five years nor his father for seven.

Meanwhile in Calcutta I developed amebic dysentery in the days before antibiotics. After recovering, at age five, my parents were advised to send me far away from contagion in the city to boarding schools in the hill country. This was a three day journey by train after which my mother kissed me farewell until the next school holidays three months away. Altogether I remained in all male boarding schools from age 5 till 18 when I was drafted into the British Army. I thrived in boarding school, excelled academically and at sports, becoming the first member of my family to go to University (Cambridge). My mother became an alcoholic and my father remained an emotionally detached but fair-minded, successful businessman.

Like Jack, I developed intellectually and physically but not emotionally. Love and how to express it were stifled in a competitive, all male environment.

Taboo

> Some gentle magnet lured me to his lap
> and coaxed my pudgy limbs and petalled skin
> inside his tweed sleeved arms. Aromas trapped
> in woolen pores rouse memories again,
> of instant pain at just the moment when
> I heard my daddy say, "You're much too grown."
> No sooner said than done, he pushed me down.

Those first grade smiles and budding social graces
were frantic recompense to fill the void
which earned me friends, but none of them replace
a forlorn sense of loss, of him annoyed,
of feeling bad inside, almost destroyed,
but never sure what error I had made,
what act of mine had made him feel afraid?

Taboo has a largely classical form with a few inconsistencies. Can you detect them? There are two 7-line stanzas with 10-syllable lines. Can you detect the rhyme scheme? It opens with a metaphor. Note that the voice is feminine, like Jack's mother, but at a very young age, sensitized and saddened from a father's lack of demonstrative affection. The three children of my first marriage endured this lack at attention when I had not matured from the rigors of boarding school and was often an absentee father preoccupied with establishing my professional reputation.

Oddly enough, a favorite photograph of my present wife Kathie is of her as a young child at about the same age as the child in my poem. From her I learned to display the emotion expressed in the next poem.

Duet

Dad,
If I'm good
will I live a trillion billion years?
I wish I could.
I'm glad I'm not a girl,
they play with dumb dolls and dress up. Yuck!
Nana looks like she's sorry sometimes
and maybe Mom is too. Are you?

I wish each day was a weekend
'cause I could watch cartoons
and keep you all the time with me.
I'd paint pictures, do puzzles and play games,
specially with Mom. She lets me win.
Know what? If you're irritable or cross
it scares me. What did I do?
But when you laugh, I like it lots.
Then I laugh too.
Why did the turtle cross the road?
To get to the Shell station. See?

I know another riddle. Will you answer if I ask?
When do grownups die, and why?
Tell me,
Dad.

Adam,
You were carefully wrought, and rightly named,
The first for Mum, the final one of four for me.
Not an afterthought,
Though after you we broke the mold
Tied our tubes and called it quits.

We've been lucky, us and you.
At birth you had a single blemish,
A strawberry splotch that faded so fast
No future lover will poke fun at it.
The time we picked was good, the seventies, not the fifties.
Sons and fathers bonded better.
Your mother's milk was copious but thin
Making you a hungry runt, who needed holding.
It comes back now, as a bonus of family hugs
That will enter the generations.

You look like the milkman's child
With blonde hair and blue eyes from God knows where.
Whatever the genes transmit we won't complain,
You catch balls and balance better
Than our own clumsy hands and wobbly feet permit.

In growth and girth you are an average child,
Someone who knows hunger so well
You can stop eating in mid-cookie.
Both parents are too busy to bribe you
With unnecessary ice cream to eat unwanted cabbage.

At two we tested wills;
One parent was good at limits, the other love.
Line-treading between indulgence and independence
We came out right this time.
Nana says you don't respect the rights of elders
But you know your own, and that's better.

You were four and fed up with coy queries
Whether your aunt's baby would be a boy or girl.
Impish, you asked if it might be a medium?
At five the three most important things you said
Were liking yourself,
Getting lots of sleep (so as not to be grouchy)
And knowing God was stronger than anybody.
Echoes or your own ideas?

Is anything original, even sin?
Added up, it's turned out well,
So far.
But all the accidents of upbringing that work
Don't drown the pit-stomach future fears of
Child molesters, malignant cells, drunk drivers and divorce.
Soon you'll be in latency, a limbo
Between Oedipus and adolescence,
A boy with a token doll
Waiting for your glands to work.

Creating the chemicals,
Exciting the world outside our windows,
Urging the species
To separate. To mate.
Go gently then, but come back later in our lives
Adam.

Duet is a free-form poem with a spontaneous structure involving a child and adult male voice. Is the content and dialog convincing? Does it move you? Compare and contrast the form of the earlier poem, *Taboo*, with *Duet*. To what extent do you feel that the different forms of these poems match their content?

Wounded Healers

Infants born in orphanages,
torn from a mother's breast,
die from a drought of love.

Kids abandoned or abused
at home, or sent safe away
from bombs or city germs
are also divorced from love.

First they cry, then wonder why?
When feelings fade ideas intrude;
they ponder what to do,
ask what conditions love,
if self is not enough?

What soothes an aching void?
Kids compensate, choose who to be:
social workers, nurses, doctors,
care providers for a world of want.
Tendering kindness for kindred souls,
solace for unmet needs,
"Mother Love" by other names.

Late in life some burn out,
giving what they went without,
wounded, healing others, not themselves.

I knew from an early age that I wanted to be a doctor; perhaps first when my mother allowed me to treat the corns and bunions in her feet with colored paint. After I became one, involved in recruiting and training medical students, I noted admissions committees tended to prefer candidates who "always knew they wanted to be a physician." I learned from the literature this was sometimes the fruit of a poisoned tree. Physicians who became impaired late in their careers due to drugs or alcohol came from troubled childhoods. This gave me pause: my mother had been an alcoholic and my incarceration in boarding school from age five was not exactly normal. Maternal deprivation has harsh consequences at whatever age. Infants confined in orphanages from birth often die of what is called anaclitic depression. After retirement, having dodged that bullet, I wrote *Wounded Healers.*

What do you notice about the structure and word choices in this poem? Several classical features are present in an irregular manner. What helps or hinders the poems message? What central theme is represented in four of the five stanzas?

HUMOR & SATIRE

Doubles Trouble

Mascular-Feminate
Masters & Johnson mate
Folk who've forgotten what
Needs to be done.

There are some who get worse,
Polymorphousperverse,
They never discover
Sex can be fun.

The double dactyl is a humorous poetic form akin to the limerick but more rigid and difficult to write. Each stanza is four lines long, and the last lines of each must rhyme. The first line of the first stanza is a repetitive nonsense word, as is the second line of the second stanza. Both the first word of the first stanza and the second word of the second stanza must have six syllables and neither of them can be repeated. The last emphatic line of each stanza has only four syllables. The second line of the first stanza should have capitalized nouns.

Poets Anthony Hecht and Paul Pascal created this form in 1951. Many were published in *Esquire* magazine. My poem was published in 1986 in the *Journal of Irreproducible Results* – a medical version of *The Onion*, devoted to satire and tongue-in- cheek medical matters. Those of you who are poets might try to test your skills against this tongue twister of a form!

Without Doubt Beyond Reason

Is faith a truth,
God's planted seed,
Or psychic fruit
Of human need?

Some seek facts
And reason to believe.
Others find conviction
Easier to achieve.

Works don't find
The key to heaven's gate.
Unbelievers good or kind
Are doomed to wait.

When in doubt
Skeptics are rejected,
Those without
More readily accepted.

After retirement I attended a Catholic Seminary for four years in search of my spiritual life. I enrolled in a Master's program for lay students alongside celibate seminarians, taught by priests and women in midlife seeking credentials to find parish work to ameliorate the priest shortage. I quit after I realized I was "spiritually handicapped."

Without Doubt Beyond Reason was written some years later, poking gentle fun at a topic many others struggle with. Its form is classical with 4-line stanzas and an alternate-line rhyme scheme. There are two exceptions; can you detect them? Each line has between three and seven syllables giving it rather a terse, didactic tone. This poem reflects a capacity for true faith which, to those who believe in God, is a rare and precious gift. My own innate skepticism was shaped by growing up in a predominately atheist culture and a profession that is empirically and scientifically based.

Fishy

Tofu of the sea,
its diminutive describes
what it must not be.

Fishy is a Haiku. The first line is a metaphor—fresh fish is free from smell with the consistency of tofu. As soon as it deteriorates it becomes inedible. The second line has alliteration while the first and third lines rhyme. These are idiosyncratic additions to a style in which "anything goes" as embellishments to the 17 syllables.

Sole Mates

Socks lead
Sad lives,
Identical twins
Forced apart.
Never sure
If they are
Left or right.
Laced inside
Dark shoes,
Stifled by
Sweaty odors,
Holey from
Torn toenails,
Darned by needles.
When one is lost
In the wash
Then its mate is
Tossed in the trash.

Doing the laundry is one of my occasional household chores. Where and why socks occasionally become estranged and disappear is an unsolved mystery, a fit topic for a poem. Perhaps the short staccato lines remind you of a washing machine relentlessly spinning from which one sock escapes, clever as Houdini, leaving a partner to its fate. *Sole Mates* is a free form poem without stanzas or rhyme but some assonance.

Used Up

Shelf fresh and shiny,
Eye appealing,
Stretched plump,
Seductive as a ripe plum,
Cozy in the palm
Urgent to be squeezed.

Twisted and wrinkled,
Brutally furled,
Bent at the end.
Uncapped and empty
Congealed and tacky,
Garbage can ready.

Used Up might be considered a hybrid form. Classical in the sense that it has two six-line stanzas but the syllables per line vary and the tone depends not on rhyme but on both alliteration and assonance. Can you spot examples of both these features? Note a stark difference in the emotional tone of the two stanzas – the first, cheerful the second sad. What object is the subject of this poem?

Genomic Eugenics

God's architectural plan
for making man
from genes
now stands revealed.
Divine mistakes can be repealed.
We know the mode
that replicates
selected templates,
corrects the errors
and eradicates
the imperfections
in His faulty code.
Rightly aligned, certain chromosomes
make canines kind.
Inserted in our genome
traditional emotion
would be converted
to unconditional devotion.
Then happy smiles
plus wagging tails
could duplicate the joy,
but grimmer folks
who don't enjoy a joke
won't hesitate.
They'll amputate!

Frustrated in its search for biological markers to illuminate the diagnosis or specific treatment of disorders that psychiatrists see, science is turning more and more towards genetics as a source of understanding.

Genomic Eugenics, a humorous free-form poem, with satire in its tail, incorporates sporadic end- and off-rhymes as well as assonance. The short lines and scant syllables give it a didactic thrust—a professor tutoring his students.

DOC doc

There's a prison doc I know well
with a bedside manner from hell.
To feelings he's blind
whatever their kind.
He tends bodies but never minds.

DOC = *Department of Corrections*

This Limerick, *DOC doc*, follows the typical form with one exception. As usual, the first, second, and fifth lines each have eight syllables; the third and fifth are shorter with just five. The traditional end-rhyme scheme should mimic the syllable count but in this instance deviates because the last line rhymes with the one before and not with the first and second. The reason is twofold – the absence of a ready rhyme for "well" and "hell." But the payoff is a *double entendre:* he doesn't care (mind) about his patient's mental health (mind).

The last four years of my career, post formal retirement, was working as the only psychiatrist in a women's prison caring for that half of the population suffering from some form of mental illness. My medical colleague seemed to delight in depriving or denying inmates any kind of psychotropic drugs he considered either too expensive or potentially addictive. I felt comfortable meeting the legitimate needs of women long deprived of appropriate mental health care, all under close supervision.

Panacea

The mind accepts what's working well,
But resurrects our body's ills
In rituals of colored pills.

White oils the joints, green quells bad moods,
Pink stifles aches, red thins the blood,
Blue re-creates a gero-stud.

Despite these drugs, death reaches all.
God pulls the plug and wills us each
eternal peace without the pills.

This satirical poem, *Panacea*, emanates from a career-long interest in psychopharmacology including, early on, a two-year stint as the Director of Psychotropic Drug Research for a pharmaceutical company. Despite the FDA, there remain many pills on the market that are little more than placebos or panaceas, including some that are legitimately labeled as drugs for anxiety and depression.

The poem has a classical form – not necessarily one that is in common use. There are three stanzas. each of three lines, each line having eight syllables. Despite that, each line is shorter than the one before, which gives the poem a symmetrical appearance on the page that is pleasing. There are various end and inside rhymes as well as some alliteration and assonance.

Mutant Sonnet

Life's Rosetta stone, the double helix
Kept the secret of its hieroglyphics
Within a spiral code, until unfurled,
The pairs of matching molecules revealed
Its building blocks and templates of the mind
In elegant simplicity aligned,
Transcribing messages on RNA
That replicates the past today.
Before the syntax of the cell is known
Impatient scientists who try to clone
Another Hemingway, a new Shakespeare,
May breed instead a mutant demagogue. I fear
Genetic engineers will play roulette
Like monkeys spelling with the alphabet.

Mutant Sonnet is a second poem about genetics. But the earlier *Genetic Eugenics* is in free form while this is a classical sonnet. Both poems end on a satirical note but this one not only has a classic form but it contains a more detailed description of the genome. Perhaps this helped it be accepted for publication in *Perspectives in Biology and Medicine* (Vol. 50, No. 1, 1986). Compare and contrast these two poems. Which do you like the best and why?

The Golden Years

We who have aged,
outgrown a misspent youth,
are oft portrayed as
sage, mellow or **serene**,
when, in reality,
moody, touchy or **mean**
reveal a harsher truth.

Golden Years, a short 7-line free-form poem, sits elegantly on the page and makes its satirical point in a single sentence with the help of only two irregularly spaced end rhymes. Written at the age of 71, it may be even truer at my present age of 82! What do you think of it?

TRAVEL & PLACES

When my father was born in 1900, the Wright brothers were still earthbound. Not until the middle of the 20th century did air travel become safe, affordable, and available to the average citizen. Flight has had a checkered history from its early days as a pampered and luxurious interlude to the contemporary cramped and uncomfortable experience. Milwaukee provides a fascinating case history of that transition. In 1978, Kimberly Clark Corporation took advantage of the Airline Deregulation Act to expand and convert its small fleet of corporate jets, used by employees to visit its mills, to form "Midwest Express." For the public at large this came with the motto, *The Best Care in the Air*, a claim supported by two-aside leather seating, gourmet meals on starched white tablecloths with china, real cutlery, and warm chocolate chip cookies, cooked on board.

Fifteen months after its virgin flight, the airline experienced its first and only fatal incident when Midwest Flight 105 crashed shortly after takeoff, killing everyone on board. Enrolled in my first poetry class at UWM, we were to write a poem in which its form on the page matched its content.

Countdown from Takeoff

They flew an arc before they met the earth
Clad in metal sheets and tender skins,
Held by tendons, bolts, ribs and struts.

Pounding hearts and powerless jets,
Welded into clumps of
Flesh and tarnished steel.

A ruddy gray
Collage on
Fresh green
Fields.

With this unique and complex form, *Countdown from Takeoff* has the jet crashing on the page with each line decreasing by one syllable, starting at 10, ending with one. The word choices mix anatomical (skins, tendons, ribs, hearts) with structural features (sheets, bolts, struts, steel, jets). A forceful impact is conveyed by the adjectives (tender, pounding, powerless) and the carnage is described in form (welded clumps) and color (collage of red, gray and green). The tone of the poem is heightened by alliteration and assonance (tender, tendons, tarnished; flesh, fresh, fields; met, metal; sheets, skin, struts, jets) and by the rhymes between the first words (flesh, fresh, fields) and the last word of the last line of the second stanza (steel) with the last two words of the third stanza (green fields).

Put aside all these details, and return to the fundamental question: what is the emotional impact of the whole poem? How much does that owe to the overall placement on the page and how much to the word choices?

Despite this tragedy, Midwest Express went on to become a highly successful and popular airline, serving twenty-one cities with nonstop flights and receiving more awards for exceptional cabin service than any other US airline from *Conde Nast Traveler* magazine. All that would change after September 11, 2001 when Midwest Flight 7 from New York to Dayton was in a near mid-air collision with hijacked United Airlines Flight 175 one minute before it hit the South Tower. Two months later my wife and I made a previously planned trip to New York on a Midwest flight and visited the devastation at Ground Zero.

Phone Home

Cell phones silenced
By crushed concrete,
Fractured steel,
Falling dust and ash.

Images fester,
Infesting minds.
Hearts tremble
Awash with fear.

Folks respond,
Finding comfort,
Bonding to friends
And calling home.

Almost every adult carried a cell phone in 2001, including many trapped and doomed in the twin towers, crushed or still able to communicate. It is impossible to calculate the sorrow, loss, hope or relief transmitted between loved ones, friends and relatives during those terrible hours. *Phone Home* seeks to tell that stark story. Its structure is hybrid; three stanzas, each having four lines with a terse three to five syllables. The first two stanzas convey the worst, the last some comfort. All three stanzas invoke alliteration and the last has the only rhyme (respond, bond).

November First

Seven weeks post nine-eleven,
Marathon runners, Diamondbacks
And curious out-of-towners
Crowd the canyons of New York.

Some come looking for new heroes,
Patriotism on their sleeves,
Others to help repair the sabotage
With caring hearts and open wallets.

Voyeurs atop the Empire State
Gaze across an urban collage,
Southward, toward ground zero,
Made vague by distance and haze.

Kamikaze cabs, (terrorists in training?),
Careen crazily downtown,
Shedding their fares in posh places
Where spending is spectator sport.

At Saint John's (clothes, not holy folks)
A blue-suited Memphis man
Watches his daughter, no bulge in sight,
Model impeccable twinsets.

Uncomplaining and indulgent
Dad pays, wondering whether
"Full alert" or anthrax unleashed
Means more money, less time remaining?

November First is a hybrid poem with six 4-line stanzas, each with variable syllables and no rhyme scheme. But there are sporadic rhymes and alliteration or assonance throughout. How many can you find? I total five rhymes in four of the stanzas and ten examples of alliteration or assonance, one or more present in each stanza.

Nine-eleven sounded the death knell of comfortable travel for the masses. Fuel prices rose, travel shrank and Midwest fell victim to takeovers; gourmet meals were long gone, only chocolate chip cookies remained. In 2012, the *Milwaukee Journal Sentinel* explained that "The cookie has crumbled" to be replaced by Animal Crackers for which customers paid a dollar. But my career still presented opportunities for travel. Educational organizations combined tax deductible trips with tours abroad. In return for lectures my wife and I travelled free.

Pharaoh's People

This
is a place
of sand and
smells, scratching
membranes and seeping
into skin folds, nooks and
crannies. Everything crumbles,
dwellings are ramshackle sheds. So
people laugh a lot and put their hope
in the life hereafter. The pharaohs did
it divinely. Their impudence commanded the
pyramids and sphinx. Willing subjects toiled in
massive servitude for nothing now. Only the promise
of resurrection and God Osiris to give safe passage to the
other side. So they could slave again as servants of the king.

Then
came a
time of decay
and desecration.
Memphis shrank to
adobe huts among the
date palms and mud colored
stains on the desert. Sand
silted the tops of their homes.
Pharaoh's bribes and comforts to ease
the voyage to eternity were dust consumed,
defiled by thieves, put on display. His barge
to reach the sun hangs suspended in a shed. Five
Pounds a peak. Unswaddled mummies were bacteria infected
and burnt. Today the dwindling dug-up assets are explained to
tourists by a new hieroglyphic. The graffiti of light and sound.

These
are a people
not readily discouraged.
The papyrus reed and the
lotus flower still bloom in the
Valley of the Nile. Pharaoh's subjects
don't complain they were misled. Nobody in
this country speaks ill of the dead. Instead
poverty is softened by all-time smiles. Endless street
greetings make even aliens feel safe. When spring holiday comes
crowds picnic at Pharaoh's tomb under tablecloth tents. Nowadays
faith is where it belongs, with Islam, and perseverance is spent on
bargaining or baksheesh. The people don't build pyramids anymore.

Each of the three stanzas of *Pharaoh's People is* a pyramid, not all of the same size. This is a unique form chosen to match the poem's theme on the page, like the earlier *Countdown*. Other structural features hardly seem relevant and the only question is how does it work for the reader? The poem's content reflects our impressions during a trip to Egypt and the Nile, including the friendly native folks we encountered and the historical as well as spiritual meaning of the pyramids. When I attempted to place the poem in more traditional ways on the page it did not seem to convey the same feelings, losing its impact and message. What do you think?

Holy Land

This is thirsty land,
strewn with rocks and bones,
layer upon layer
of truth and faith,
told by relics and holy ruins.

This is blood soaked ground
fed when ancient armies
fought at Megiddo;
here knights and martyrs
shed life for new beliefs.

This is fertile soil
where twisted olive trees,
Millennia old,
cast friendly shade
upon the Son of God.

This is sandy shore,
here pilgrims gather,
I and others,
seeking footprints
left behind, long before.

In 1999, while a lay student at the Catholic Seminary, I sought
to bolster my meager faith by joining a group of 42 pilgrims including
five family members led by the pastor of our local church, a published
multi-lingual author of books about Hebrew and Christian history.
Our pilgrimage covered Syria, Jordan and Israel, including the Holy
Land. It was a time of relative political calm so we were able to visit
all the key religious and historical sites. Among them were the Dead
Sea, Sea of Galilee (here Jesus preached the Beatitudes), Qumran
(The Dead Sea Scrolls), the River Jordan (baptism), Megiddo (aka
Armageddon, site of the mythical battle between good and evil),
Capharneaum and Nazareth (focus of Jesus's ministry), Cesarea
(Paul's missionary trips), the Mount of Olives (Judas's betrayal), the
Via Dolorosa (the crucifixion), the Wailing Wall, the Church of the
Holy Sepulcher and the Citadel (Holy sites for Jews, Christians, and
the Orthodox Greek Church).

Holy Land is brief and pithy; only four stanzas, each with five
lines of variable length. For the first three stanzas there is no rhyme
scheme or classical features. It relies for its impact on adjectival
imagery (rocks and bones, relics of holy ruins, blood soaked ground,

ancient armies, twisted olive trees, fertile soil, friendly shade, sandy shore). The last stanza contains the only rhyme (shore, before) and its last two lines capture the purpose of the pilgrimage in a lyrical alliterative metaphor, "seeking footprints / left behind, long before."

In these last two poems and in the ones to come, it is important to note that they appeared spontaneously on the page in the form you see them now. The analysis of how the form works to convey its message is entirely *post hoc,* as it were, an intellectual 'autopsy' of a creative event.

India Redux

This India is,
and yet is not,
the place where I grew
from four to nine years old.
Transported by sea,
then trapped by war.
With peace declared
my father and the Raj
went home to England,
leaving Muslims and Hindus
to vent their sacred rage.
The jewel was sliced apart,
the British Crown thrown out,
Mahatma Gandhi sacrificed,
New India's gentle Oedipus.

In Calcutta, Chowringee
remains a honking concourse
dividing banyan trees and cricketers
from crumbling concrete.
The Grand Hotel still stands,
owned now by Oberoi,
ornate as memory tells it stood
in nineteen-thirty-eight.
Inside, modern trends intrude:
jalapeno poppers, not cocktail canapes,
margaritas, not pink gin,
discotheques, not string quartets,
polite address now *sir*, not *sahib*.

In Darjeeling,
India's ceiling to the world,
tea gardens still glisten green
on the slopes of Tiger Hill.
But the boarding school
I was banished to,
a refuge from city dysentery,
has vanished.
This time a new bug
travels with me
to Hotel Windermere,
keeping me in bed
before the same coal fire
that warmed my mother
when she dropped me off,
kissed, then said "good bye"
for three months, more or less.

In India now, everywhere,
things are mostly as they were.
Old monuments to Mogul power,
seething masses in poverty,
a brown spectrum of humanity.
Sacred cows, hens, stray curs and pigs
crammed in dusty streets,
one multicolored blur of cloth,
flesh, feather, skin and hide,
pressed close to mother earth
and tightly knit together.

My present differs from my past
but India's child is much the same.

In 2002, my wife, Kathie, and youngest son, Adam, joined me on a trip to India to visit all the places I knew as a child. Included were my father's business offices in Calcutta where we met his Indian successor who invited us to cocktails at the Grand Hotel and the hill stations where the boarding schools I went to once were situated. At the Windermere Hotel in Darjeeling (within sight of Mount Everest) we fortuitously met the wife of my father's former co-director in Pakistan; years previously she and her husband had spent time with my parents in England.

India Redux is free-form with four stanzas of irregular length and a concluding doublet. The first stanza is historical, dealing with India's independence from the British Empire and murder of Gandhi, its leader. The second stanza portrays the changes in urban Calcutta, while the third deals with the hill station Darjeeling, within sight of Mount Everest, ending with the covert angst of boarding school. The final stanza uses colorful imagery and itemization of its components to convey the unchanging nature of rural India.

Tango

Porta La Plat has a craw
wide enough to swallow
the sailors of the world,
lured ashore by the whores
of Buenos Aires.

Here men pluck guitars
to a carnal beat.
Gender innuendo
throbs to the tempo
of an Argentine tango.

Autocrats in tuxedos
stole the duet,
swapped the sailor's slut
to strut and glide
with scant-clad Madonnas.

There is rhythm and desire
in gesture and glance
posture that speaks
primal fantasies
of must or chance, love or lust.

Its beat is unrelenting,
but everyone knows
the tango is ending
to the sound of a sailor's
drowned feelings.

Fado

The Portuguese today
know centuries of sorrow,
once captains of the ocean,
owners of an Empire,
now washed away.

Slim coastal strip, Iberia's face,
fertile, fecund, domain,
once invaded and defiled
by envious neighbors,
now regained.

Grapes, olives, almonds,
grow in shale and shallow soil
on dizzy sun-burned slopes,
ripe fruits in terraced rows,
picked clean by calloused hands.

Fall harvest's home,
hard labor done.
Across the nation
the melancholic Fado
is sung in celebration.

Tango and Fado share a common classical form with 5 line stanzas of irregular lengths. Both employ rhyme, assonance and alliteration in a sporadic manner. More importantly both share a common theme – a nationally known musical form, the tango and fado, a feature that is reflected in the rhythm of the poems. This contrasts with the free form-nature of *India Redux*. There is an interesting analogy that can be made between musical and poetic forms. Indian music is based on the *raga*, a series of only five to nine notes on which a melody is constructed by the way the notes are rendered and the mood they convey. Ragas can also vary by time of day, the seasons, or prevailing mood. So the raga is a melodic framework for improvisation – much like free-form poetry. In contrast, classical music involves a written score of notations that encourages conformity, much like classical poetry.

While *India Redux* appeared on the page in free form and both *Tango* and *Fado* arrived in a classic form, this analogy to the musical forms employed by the three cultures is *post hoc.* In both poetry and music there is discretion about the extent to which a poet or musician chooses to improvise, often influenced by the theme or topic.

Panama Canal

Over three decades and more
thirty thousand died to join
the quadrants of the compass,
East to West and sea to sea.

The French failed nobly, foiled by
jungle, hard rock, death and debt,
leaving just a half-dug trench.

Next, the Yankees toiled like moles,
shifting tons of sod and soil,
stifling deadly disease,
blasting through a mountain chain,
damming rivers, flooding the trench.

Fifty miles of lake, cuts, locks
made the Panama Canal,
opened on the eve of war.

Today it conveys vessels
of the world in peaceful trade.

The subject matter of each of the three preceding poems was derived from cruise ships to South America, Portugal, and Panama. The relationship between poet and subject matter differed; it was far more intimate traversing the canal than going ashore. Perhaps for this reason *Panama Canal* felt closer to the implications of the place.

It was completed and opened just two weeks before the "Great War" was declared in 1914 between Britain, France, and Germany. Two years later the Battle of the Somme raged across twenty miles of slit trench and 300,000 troops were killed in five months, ten times the number who died from accidents, malaria, and yellow fever during thirty years of digging the fifty miles of trench to create the Panama Canal. In both France and Panama many of those who died were buried close by the trench they helped dig. In more than a century since its completion the Panama Canal has provided safe passage to more than a million ships.

Ode to Merrie England

England is a lovely land,
filled with friendly chaps.
On the other hand . . .

The toilets never flush
enough to wash
your turds away!

Public loos charge users fees;
at Harrods in the city
it costs a pound to pee.
(It used to be a penny).

Air conditioning's a window plus a fan,
which makes for sweaty sex
that wrecks your nuptial plan.

We love the pubs, the bitter beer
and dishes which they sell,
like fish and chips.

Steer clear of posher places
that bill for bottled water;
tap water oughta do.

Yes, England is a lovely land,
filled with friendly chaps,
on the other hand . . .

Take a Yank's advice,
don't push the Brits too far,
never ask for ice!

Annual visits to my brother and a best friend in England inured me to the idiosyncrasies of our different cultures. But I remain enough of a fan of my birthplace's crude humor that I am occasionally tempted to emulate it. By now the reader will be sufficiently tutored in an ability to comment on the form and characteristics of a poem to comment on *Ode to Merrie England* and its success or otherwise in making a point.

NATURE

Lake Effect

Tepid steam
rising
from ice flows,
a bronze sun
glistening
on frigid snow,
barren branches
spawning
newborn icicles.
Divine alchemy
forging
God's gold.

This poem, *Nature*, emerged on a winter morning, walking my black lab. Stanley by frozen Lake Michigan as the sun was rising above the horizon. The form is vertical, narrow to mimic the sun's rays that are carried earthwards by four rhyming gerunds (rising, glistening, spawning, forging) each separated by two descriptive lines, leading to the climax of divine purpose.

Camp Out

This waterlogged weekend
pent-up kids and tent-trapped grownups
incubate cabin fever under
shrinking canvas, dripping like
a ticking clock into soggy ground.

Parents cluster like damp crows
round a smoking campfire,
cawing their garden fence chat,
cloakroom jokes and gossip
that kills time and office enemies.

One fresh-scratched girl says
climbing fences is a waste of skin,
except how else can she get to
exciting places that say **KEEP OUT**
when they invite her in.

Two scrawny boys swap
penis tales and sexy stories,
giggling and bragging, each
knows best how to make his prick
stiff and tall, like a giraffe's neck.

A madder'n' hell Mom stacks
muddied jeans and puddled shoes,
cussing kids and idle dads,
wishing she'd packed sparklers,
marshmallows and more Band-Aids.

On sunny Monday morning
not a single soul admits
they quit their sodden site
and scurried home to dry suburbia
earlier than they usually do.

In mid-life we owned a VW camper with a pop-up roof and bundles of nooks and crannies for storing everything needed for a weekend trip to a nearby state park. *Camp Out* is one of my favorite poems (every poet has them) because of its descriptive power. It is loaded with metaphors, especially the first two stanzas which set the tone, as well as vivid imagery throughout. There is also plenty of assonance (muddied, puddled), alliteration (sodden site, scurried, suburbia) as well as unexpected rhymes (prick, neck, suburbia, earlier). The final stanza tells how we always enjoyed ourselves even when we didn't.

Seminary Cemetery

Two hundred eighty-one women
in consecrated ground.
Lined like veterans,
named and dated
under humble headstones.
All born and dead,
unemancipated,
between two councils.

Men are in short supply,
scattered sparsely about,
each lying alone
beneath marble monuments
with etched eulogies.
Their proud tombstones
fractured or toppled over
by teenage gangs.

Looking on, God wonders
why she gave them genders.

The Catholic seminary cemetery I attended stood in many acres of woods. In the midst was a neglected last resting place for nuns and priests who served their maker more than a century ago. The historic misogyny and chauvinism of the catholic hierarchy was covert and stifled but ever present. The two 8-line stanzas of *Seminary Cemetery* contain some alliteration but no rhymes until the final doublet which carries the message.

Flowers for Life

This garden is my gift,
planted for you.
Fragrant and perennial
from spring through fall,
Hellebore to Columbine,
Valentine's till Sweetest day
an annual recollection
of lives entwined.

Herbs to kiss your lips,
scents to flood your senses,
weeds to remind us
love best be blind
to imperfection.
When we are joined forever
it will remain,
our gift to others.

When our youngest child emancipated, we moved from our elegant home with its tiny garden to a bungalow standing in half an acre of neglected yard. I set about designing an English garden and watched it mature and blossom over the years.

Flowers for Life was written to my wife on Sweetest Day and published in *Labors of Love* by Noble House in 2005. Another hybrid form (my favorite genre) with unusual end rhymes between lines in the different stanzas. Can you spot them? There are two, plus one metaphor and some alliteration in the second.

Early Spring

A slow melt
strips the bare earth
of cold skin,
naked to a shiny sun
that breaks its
mellow shafts
on furrowed ridges
of frigid soil.

Somewhere below,
thirsty seeds swell,
bursting from
a parched winter,
breaking blind
toward the trickling light.
       Tonight a
       frost might come.

Early Spring is a partner to *Lake Effect*, later in the season, but birthed in similar circumstances – Stanley's early morning walk. Its characteristics are similar (you might like to compare them) but the ending affect is the polar opposite, given added emphasis by setting off the last two lines as a rhyming doublet (as in the sonnet form).

God's Quilt

Harvest gold
Sown between
Green turf
and tilled
Brown earth.

God's Quilt is the shortest poem in my oeuvre, 12 syllables. Like a Haiku this metaphor is in a form that packs a punch. What characteristics help the poem succeed?

Requiem for Stanley

Stanley came the way most dogs do,
A puppy, begged for by my son,
Bequeathed back when walking him
Became too big a burden
For a busy child to bear.

Pure black Lab, bred to fetch back
Sticks, bones, balls or Frisbees.
Stanley's Arctic island genes
Custom made him for his daily swims
In our icy northern lake.

Tightly muscled, an ornery alpha dog,
Stanley perfumed lamp posts, fire hydrants,
Tree stumps, garbage cans, and parked cars.
Cocking his leg even when
His tank was on empty.

Stanley had the appetite of an elephant,
The table manners of a two-year-old,
The menu of a starving goat,
A mouth like a vacuum cleaner
And iron-clad innards.

A disgusting significant other,
Stanley passed gas without guilt,
Ate cat shit and smiled,
Stole my supper from the kitchen table,
Teased me with torn socks and chewed shoes.

Stanley liked to lick my naked toes,
Unleashing feelings not linked
To sex, skin color or bribery.
If people had tails or wagged their faces
There'd be fewer divorces.

Seventeen years of loyalty and love
Have left an aching void,
Bereft of walks, licks, barks, or laughs.
Only his ghost and scattered ashes
Guard Stanley's much beloved yard.

Requiem for Stanley is another of my favorite poems, not as much for the poetic form but because of the sentiments it expresses and the memories it evokes. But how does it work for someone who never knew Stanley, or who may not be a dog lover? If it works for you at the aesthetic level is there any need to dissect the mechanics? The poem has a classic form of seven stanzas, each of five lines, but of unequal length and without end rhymes. There are classical features scattered throughout the poem but are they noteworthy? Stanza one has 8 words beginning with the letter "b" (alliteration). Stanza four employs multiple metaphors in describing Stanley's eating habits. Stanza five has an unusual end rhyme – "chewed shoes" (assonance). Stanza seven also has assonance – walks, licks, barks. If one removed these features surgically how would you feel about what remains?

Cathedral

Pin drop echoes
Of organ pomp,
Slow files
Of hooded monks,
In metered steps
With muffled chant,
Shuffling
Down wind tunnels
Of frigid stone.

Brute sepulcher
Of quarried slabs
Mute columns
That prop apart
Vaulted roof
From flagstone floor.
Bleak altar
Worn flat
By pilgrims' prayer.

Architecture is part of the landscape which impinges on or blends with nature (especially if you are of the Frank Lloyd Wright School). *Cathedral* has two stanzas of nine lines each, but with few syllables per line, giving it a narrow, erect posture on the page. In what way does the word choice convey the atmosphere for a place of worship? Does it feel like a cathedral? Would you want to pray or meditate there? Why or why not?

Late Harvest

Prayer is a want
God plants at birth,
But unmet needs,
A drought of love
Force weeds to grow.

Our haste to speak,
Our introspection,
Our must-control,
Our self-perfection,
Our lack of trust.

These faults that nip
The buds of faith
Yield no crops, just
Silence between
God and us.

Despite these doubts,
We will keep vigil.
Divine seeds sprout;
What God has sown
He means to reap.

Late Harvest might be equally well placed in the later section on Spirituality but three of its four stanzas use nature, the harvest, as a metaphor. The second stanza uses the oratorical strategy of repetition to provide emphasis but it also includes assonance (haste, trust, must) and rhyme (introspection, perfection; must, trust). The final stanza has both an end rhyme (doubts, sprout) and an inside rhyme (keep, reap). Overall do you think the metaphor speaks to you? Why or why not?

Mind Seed

Words or flowers,
Syllables or petals,
Pen or spade?

Tilling fantasy,
Planting metaphors,
Feeding imagination.

Pruning rhyme,
Clipping alliteration,
Weeding line breaks.

Sun or showers,
Asleep or awake,
Verse germinates.

Ruminating about my twin hobbies, gardening and poetry, I realized each was a metaphor for the other. Seeds are cultivated by spade and ideas by pen before germinating in soil or on the page. Just as plants grow buds, flowers and petals, nourished by sun and rain, so poems acquire words, metaphors and syllables formed in daily solitude or nighttime reverie. As plants need to be trimmed, pruned or fertilized, poems require attention to rhyme, alliteration, and line breaks.

Mind Seed says as much or more than the above prose paragraph in far fewer (less than a third) words. Do you agree? Which do you prefer, poem or prose?

MENTAL HEALTH MATTERS

My career as a psychiatrist lasted from 1962, when I began residency training at the Maudsley Hospital and Institute of Psychiatry in London and ended 46 years later after I retired (for the second time) in 2008. The full story is told in my memoir, *Bits and Pieces of a Psychiatrist's Life* (XLibris, 2012), but what follows is a selection of poems written beginning in mid-career, after 1980, when I moved to Milwaukee at age 46.

Birth Choices

Birthmother

This is the product of our conception
That multiplies in fluid nurtured gloom
Outlasting love, growing to perception
Unwanted but protected in its womb.
Shall we destroy what we so briefly wrought?
Before our secret reaches other eyes?
Or shall we parent it ourselves? And ought
We live the lesson of our loving lies?
It could be cheaply done and quickly gone,
Scraped clean and emptied out within a week.
There's no real pain they say, this early on.
No one will know and even we won't speak.
   But unsure lives ought never end another,
   We should seek a loving barren mother.

Adoptive Mother

You were born to us without conception,
The unloved product of another womb.
Can this longed-for heir to our reception
Be so deformed to make us search for whom
To blame: your twisted genes or our dry hearts?
Were we too hopeful of our good intent?
Will extra effort mend your broken parts?
Make you the child of whom we dreamt?
When parents, brothers, sisters, church and schools
All fail to curb your hurt or build your trust?
Can tender limits, pleas or tougher rules
Give birth to love? Or lacking it we must
        Surrender you to what the world will do
        Because we nurtured you and nothing grew.

The Child

A full term failure of contraception
I was implanted in an alien womb.
I don't care who fucked whom. The deception
Taught me early on, there is no real room
In life for me. Dry breasts and unsure hands
Told me the rest. I somehow got the sense
Of early transience, like one-night stands.
I grew to be a token recompense
Who fed your middle-class nobility
And purged your conscience of its social sins.
I even cured your infertility
So your real kids could grow in white-clad skins.
        You wonder why I feel so black and small
        That I might one day want to end it all?

The seeds of *Birth Choices* germinated early in my poetic career from several different sources. Patients sometimes sought my advice about adoption and I was familiar with the genetic uncertainties involved. At the same time, one of my Caucasian colleagues lived in an ethnically integrated neighborhood where he and his wife had adopted and were successfully raising several Afro-American children. Another friend's wife, walking in her neighborhood park, was pistol whipped and raped by a young black man, requiring over a hundred stiches to her face. This tragic event may have metaphorically transformed itself into the sentiments expressed in my poem.

The form is a classical sonnet but it is an unusual triplet in three stanzas, each with a different voice: a perplexed and uncertain birth mother, a frustrated and disappointed adoptive mother and, finally, an angry and self-destructive child. Altogether it is a disturbing poem that probably transmits and stirs strong emotions in the reader that I invite you to express. Which of the three stanzas moves you the most? Why? Note that the last stanza has the unusual feature of several inside rhymes. What, if anything, does this contribute to your thoughts or feelings?

This, my first published poem, appeared in the local paper *Crazy Shepherd* (December, 1984). The paper later changed its name, became *The Shepherd Express*, and ceased publishing poems.

Nature and Nurture

What matters most is
Kind hosts and loving homes for
Family chromosomes.

This Haiku, *Nature and Nurture*, appeared in 2010, a quarter century after *Birth Choices*. It deals with the foundational question in psychiatry: How much of what we see and call "mental illness" stems from genes and how much from upbringing? Perhaps this is a belated subconscious attempt to make amends for its gloomy predecessor by substituting optimism for pessimism. Note the rhyme scheme and alliteration.

Our Fathers

"The poets and philosophers before me have discovered the unconscious; I have discovered the scientific method with which the unconscious can be studied."
FREUD: Father of Psychotherapy.

Many forms of insanity are unquestionably the external manifestations of the effects upon the brain substance of poisons fermented within the body."
THUDICHUM: Father of Neurochemistry.

She wakes me up in early morning doubt.
Crazed eyes and alien name: Luz Medino.
Both fuel the need in me to know about
her persona, gene pool, Puerto Rico.

Sour culture and unruly cells enslave
her brain in bitter juice. It can't go free
slumped sad inside its melancholy cave,
bound by its own unraveled chemistry.

The day they cut her breast away she wept.
Her hardwood face dissolved in acid tears.
Except for dream-infested nights she kept
slammed shut that angry door to all her fears.

She doesn't rage against her fate. So sure
she is a devil who deserves to die
that words or drugs have not produced a cure
and Freud or Thudichum can't tell me why.

Our Fathers goes to the core of a psychiatrist's dilemma: the patient who fails to benefit from the basic tools of our trade, psychotherapy and medication. In the early years of my career (1960-1970) there was a stark contrast between the American love affair with psychoanalysis and the European belief in the biological origins of psychotic disorders. As the century progressed Freud's theories came increasingly into question and, while the new drugs held sway for several decades, they too failed to fulfill their early promise. Their speculative effects on neurotransmitters were called into doubt and they were also lacking in clinical specificity, with troubling side effects, hard to tolerate. It became increasingly clear that the causes, natural history, and outcome of mental illnesses were determined by a complex kaleidoscope of biological, social, and psychological factors, often in variable amounts.

As benefits a primitive issue, this poem appears in classical form. Four stanzas, each of four lines, all with ten syllables and a consistent scheme of alternating end rhymes. The first stanza spells out the potential origins of Luz Medino's illness: her persona (psychological), biology (gene pool) and culture (social). The second stanza elaborates on putative neurochemical manifestations and the third on an additional biological factor (breast surgery), as well as Luz's emotional responses (sadness, fear, anger and troubling dreams). The final stanza incorporates the psychotic nature of her illness, the frustrating failure to benefit from treatment, and an inability to understand the origins of her disturbed state in a way that might lead to a cure.

Readers who would like to learn more about Thudichum can visit INHN.org and click on Home, then Biographies and Thudichum, Father of Neurochemistry.

The Prison Doctor's Dilemma

In Minimum Security,
one third of women are marred
by abuse, breached boundaries,
male brutality
and psychic scars.

Mean families and broken homes
magnify each faulty gene.
Alone, burdened by childcare,
illness quickens urban angst.

When sickness is dosed with
liquor, crack, heroin or pot
prison is one wrong day away.

Inside, inmates suffer DSM disorders,
with substance abuse in forced remission,
diagnoses embroidered with penal epithets,
"malingering" or "manipulative,"
abusive echoes eclipse redemption.
Prescriptions take weeks to work,
from a formulary stripped of
expensive or "addictive" drugs.
We offer safety over swift solace.

Denied solitude or comfort
primal fears and fractured sleep
sometimes elude our panaceas.

DSM = *Diagnostic & Statistical Manual of the
American Psychiatric Association*

The Doctor's Dilemma is borrowed from George Bernard Shaw's play of the same name. First staged in 1906, it explores the moral dilemmas created by limited medical resources and conflicts between earning a livelihood and addressing the patient's needs. Shaw's protagonist Colenso Ridgeon is believed by many to be modelled on Arbuthnot Lane, surgeon to Queen Victoria, who made his fortune removing the colon for trivial and misunderstood maladies like constipation. The prison doctor is also limited by a restrictive formulary and constrained by a generous salary – I earned enough money in one ten-hour day a week to help pay my son's medical school tuition. Challenging the ideology of the system would get short shrift.

The Prison Doctor's Dilemma a free-form poem; the stanzas and lines are of unequal length but there are a few rhymes and alliterations scattered throughout. It was written early in the four years it took my son to graduate and doesn't reflect the gratification I felt about the good I was able to accomplish despite limited resources.

Many of the psychiatrists and psychologists who staffed prisons throughout the State had academic appointments in medical schools and excellent reputations. My only major disappointment and concern is expressed in the next poem.

Rehab

There's women jailed
That's done some wrong,
Whose minds have failed
And don't belong.

They broke our laws,
Got locked in cells,
Behind steel bars,
They're taking pills.

But once let out
They'll soon be back,
Revoked without
The skills they lack.

Rehab, this second prison poem, is in classic form, only three stanzas, each with four lines of four syllables and alternating end rhymes. Both these poems have a pessimistic theme but their forms could not be more different. Can you imagine why? The choice was not deliberate or consciously made but perhaps there is a covert reason.

Elevators are . . .

Elevators are elusive,
Up or down, open or shut
But not when you want one.

Elevators are toxic
To Type A temperaments,
Eager to arrive early.

Elevators are oral,
Engulfing us all
Behind closed doors.

Elevators are intimate
Like one night stands,
Too transient to wait.

Elevators are rejecting,
Emptying everyone
Out on the floor.

Elevators are faulty:
Steel vaults for bodies
Buried in basements.

Elevators is an upwardly mobile metaphor for everyday life. Fear of elevators is common among the 530 known phobias given Latin or Greek names by learned physicians but, oddly enough, this one has no name unless it is considered a subset of *claustrophobia*, fear of closed spaces. Just as asylums were built at safe distances on the periphery of towns so modern day inpatient units, like those I worked in, were often on the top floor of their hospital with the windows secured to prevent suicides.

Its success and content are related to its form on the page: erect, up and down, a stanza for each of the seven floors with a different psychic metaphor for every stop: avoidant, obsessive, oral, submissive, intimate, rejecting, fearful. Does it work for you? Do you have a fear of elevators? If so, how does it color your response to the poem?

Doubt

you wonder why I worry
well I wonder too
maybe it was dad
whose rivet gun eyes
    poked holes in your ego
        my ego I mean

sorry but images of him
    pop in and out
        expecting
        correcting
        inoculating
        my thoughts
with
        shoulds
        oughts
        and doubts

Doubt, this (very) free-form poem, was published in the UWM student *Jazz Street* (1986, Vol. 3). It uses its form and place on the page to mirror the content – a young female student explaining to her counsellor why she is so anxious. Its line breaks and lack of punctuation convey insecurity and hesitancy until its structure finally develops conformity and rigidity. She enumerates her father's dominating and demanding tactics which create her own obsessive strategies to cope with self-doubt. Note how this assumption of conformity introduces some classical features (expecting, correcting, inoculating; thoughts, oughts, doubts).

Psychosurgery

Our eyes engage.
Clenched lids
can't staunch
the flow of tears
I operate on her awake
with questions that cut
pauses that retract
for her sake

We arrive
back where it began
Her black ailing momma
... alive
Her white unwed dad
... dead
When she was five
When purebred peers
nicknamed her
... Honky
Now I see
the pale skin
the muddled genes
the almost afro hair
Now her despair
makes sense
Bereft
She wants to die
Waiting

to ask her white daddy
why he left her here
half black....   alone
Quickly I close
Sadness has spread too far

Psychosurgery was published in *Off Hours* a magazine for physicians in January 1986. It was written while I was doing therapy with a medical student of mixed ethnic heritage, hoping to become a surgeon. Also free-form, with no punctuation, erratic use of line breaks and capital letters; its place on the page assists in dramatizing the metaphor of poetry as semantic surgery. Do you think the last stanza conveys the end of a session or the termination of therapy? Why?

Rebirthing

There are many ways
To integrate and mend
A cracked persona.

Celebrate your assets,
Befriend the defects,
Meld psyche and soma.

Think and feel in synergy,
Reframe old wounds,
Unlock trapped energy.

Search for and choose
A grounding vision,
An angel in the rock.

Then walk the talk,
Shun the victim game,
Cease blaming others.

Nourish second chances,
Seek smiling faces
That nurture you anew.

Psyche and soul flourish
When faith and grace
Reunite the whole.

This hybrid poem, *Rebirthing,* has seven stanzas each with three short but uneven lines and a sporadic rhyme scheme that portrays an idealized approach to healing a wounded psyche – perhaps a recipe for several of the preceding poems and their predicaments. But it should be taken with a grain of salt in light of the next and final poem in Mental Health Matters.

Blind Insight

Shrinks think their illusions
Oughta offer solutions
When often they don't.

Taking a horse
To the water
Won't make it drink.

This two stanza poem tells the essential truth about all our efforts to influence another person's behavior. First there is insight, understanding the nature of the problem, but then the harder part – doing something about it. A truth known to every therapist and, ultimately one hopes, to each person seeking help.

SPIRITUAL DIMENSIONS

Born in Britain of two agnostic parents, I grew up in a spiritually bleak environment where churches remain almost empty, their gorgeous architecture crumbling. At my Methodist boarding school we attended chapel daily and on weekends were obliged to visit a local church of our choice – in my case the Church of England (Episcopal). I declined the rite of Confirmation and, as I matured and favored first science and then medicine, I became increasingly skeptical and adopted an epistemological frame of reference which demanded proof and validity for my increasingly atheistic mindset. This persisted throughout my career even as I inevitably became more aware of the emotional significance of the belief systems of those I sought to help. So, perhaps not surprisingly, I decided after retirement, to explore my own spiritual dimension in depth.

Married to a lifelong Catholic this led me to enroll in our Archdiocese's seminary in a program for a Master's degree in Applied Pastoral Studies (MAPS). At a leisurely pace this might take several years to acquire but I was in no hurry and the prospect was enticing. I was taught religion and philosophy by priests, mostly with doctoral degrees, in small classes that included the celibate male seminarians (I gave up medicine but not sex) as well as middle-aged women, many seeking second careers as parish administrators to relieve the priest shortage. A nun served as my spiritual director. I was quickly relieved of any idea that deeply religious folks were feeble minded and easily persuaded. Competing academically with budding priests, over twenty years younger, I was hard pressed to maintain an A grade and preserve my dignity in written and oral exams at the end of each course. Paradoxically, as I reveled in this stimulating spiritual and academic environment I gradually became more aware that I was spiritually handicapped. Others viewed faith as a gift from a God that I was unable to accept. When it was time to prepare for graduation I decided any gifts or skills I had were better deployed in a return to my profession. So I left the Seminary to work as the only psychiatrist at four clinics belonging to Catholic Charities where I saw people unable to find a psychiatrist willing to accept Medicaid reimbursement. In my spare time I developed *Faith in Recovery*, an ecumenical program in local churches for parishioners and families dealing with mental illness. This brief detour may explain the way in which the poems that follow offer differing perspectives on spirituality.

Seek and Find

Man may find God
In anxious prayer
Or maybe not.

Man may find God
In tedious work
Or maybe not.

Man may find God
In glorious work
Or maybe not.

Man may find God
In pious churches
Or maybe not.

Man may find God
In joyous play
Or maybe not.

Man may find God
In obvious places
Or maybe not.

God will find man
Somewhere he searches
and never not.

Seek and Find has a simple classical but cunning form. It gathers its strength and appeal from repetition of the first and third

lines and by the rhyme of the second word in the second line of all
seven stanzas. In the final stanza, the ambivalence I was attempting
to rid myself of is resolved, at least on paper, by switching "may" to
"will."

In the Vestibule

Thanks, but no thanks!
How come you created me this way,
An INTJ?
We "skeptics and atheists"
Who wait outside the gate?

You made me in your image
Yet we can't communicate?
I try but . . .
Chores preempt prayer,
Rumination ruins contemplation.

But wait, I dimly see . . .
The threads of God's diversity,
Woven in the tapestry of life.
I owe it to myself to use
The gifts bestowed on me.

I can find a way to pray . . .
Discern reality, not dreams,
Make work wait,
Plan quiet times
Meditate on solid themes.

Slowly, the gate opens
Just wide enough
To show my shadow side
Can this be true . . . ?
Your grace at work in me?

In the Vestibule was written while I was in the seminary and attending a national conference on the relationship between the Myers Briggs Personality Inventory and prayer life or meditation. It was attended by a wide variety of business people, human resource directors and assorted mental health professionals although I may have been the only psychiatrist studying religion.

This poem reflects my spirituality at the time – on the cusp between belief and disbelief, desperately seeking a rapprochement. Hybrid in form, it has five stanzas, each with five lines but an irregular syllable count. There are several rhymes within or between lines and stanzas.

It's As If . . .

For mankind to survive
Our primal thirst for sin and war
Takes more than the Torah
Or a single sect.

It's as if . . .
Everything Jesus said is true.
Only a universal creed
Of loving words
Will do.

It's as if . . .
Baptism did not create
An easy believer.
Culture and training
Made me a skeptic, doubter.

It's as if . . .
Christ's divinity, the resurrection,
The Trinity, Immaculate Conception,
Perpetual virginity
All feed my incredulity.

It's as if . . .
I seek to emulate
His Sermon on the Mount
Without faith, despite doubt
When deeds alone don't count.

Do you wonder why?
I try to live
The Jesus myth
As if it's true.

It's As If details sources of my ambivalence and doubt. Although it has six 5-line stanzas, they are as erratic as my ruminations in terms of syllables, line length and appearance on the page. The fourth stanza has a rich rhyme scheme, the fifth stanza has three end rhymes. The last line turns doubt on its head!

Faith

Our ancestors evolved
at a high price.
Bigger brains knew and counted
the sources of sustenance:
flesh, water, grains.
Then humankind
gained prescience,
the certainty of death.

Cave dwellers
imagined higher powers,
placating them with sacrifice,
their price for peace of mind;
quelling grief and angst
about famine, drought,
meagre supplies
and brief lives.

Greeks, Romans and Hindus
sought certainty in life
and afterlife beyond;
from pantheons of deities
with human, animal
or hybrid forms,
whose lives and fate
they sought to emulate.

The Trinity came late,
God's son a sacrifice.
The entry fee
at heaven's gate
to all eternity:
Belief, without uncertainty,
that mythic truth
called faith.

Faith contrasts an evolutionary and faith-based view of an afterlife—an attempt to stifle ambivalence?

I or We?

Our brains are wired
for altruism or desire,
layer on layer
of options, decisions,
from cortex to limbic lobe,
orchestrating a symphony
of character and persona,
generosity or greed,
compassion or cruelty,
love or lust,
trust or deceit; will it be
I or we?

Religion claims
the moral ground,
names choice, conscience.
What if survival of the fittest
prevails instead
and doing good is best
for humankind?
Without divine intervention
without the imposition of
Crusades and Inquisitions
or more *just* wars.
No deity, only we
I and thee?

Wolves don't laugh or weep
yet species evolve
when law and love trump tooth and claw.
When genocide, holocaust, homicide,
guilt, failure and despair
invoke a higher power,
answers come not from Holy writ
but in genetic code.
If both pathways transmit spiritual gifts
of hope, compassion, love and trust
Then brain and faith agree;
the future lies
not with I, but we.

Although *I or We?* has three stanzas that separate its polemical points, it is essentially free-form with a few sporadic rhymes. It is an agnostic attempt to spell out an alternative to religion by focusing not solely on personal spiritual redemption "I" but also on genetically endowed behavioral traits to save mankind, "We". The first stanza stakes a claim to the genetic origin of behavioral traits that govern human behavior. The second stanza questions whether human survival is best linked to the capacity of the genome to provide positive and benevolent behaviors contrasted with the historical, sometimes destructive, shortcomings of religious belief. The last stanza claims that the best of both religious faith and genetic code can combine to save humanity.

Question in Feminist Theology Class

"Does a Then and Now analogy allow a He and She theology?"

Early Councils dictated dogma,
leaving naught to chance,
Today's debate embraces metaphor
and celebrates nuance.

The past taught uniformity,
negating every heresy.
The present seeks inclusivity,
creating more diversity.

Patriarchy defines a heavenly faith
for Christendom from birth.
Matriarchy aligns its path toward
God's kingdom on Earth.

My wife is a strong feminist and I am an avid supporter; each of us negates the patriarchy and misogyny of the Catholic Church. So the environment at the Seminary was exciting, including as it did, many second-career women who would have preferred priesthood to parish administration. I was elected to the Student Council and pushed that agenda during the tenure of enlightened and liberal Archbishop Rembert Weakland. Towards the end of my time he retired and was replaced by Timothy Dolan, a strong conservative, designated by the press as *papabile*, a potential candidate for Pope. The last class I attended before leaving was on Feminist Theology taught by a woman theologian from Marquette University. I was the only male among about twenty women – the male seminarians, aware of the winds of change and fearful of the Archbishop's displeasure, stayed away.

This poem, based on an ancient controversy, is in an appropriately classical form. Each of the three stanzas has two sentences and four lines with end rhymes between second and last line. The content conveys the contrast between a "top down" patriarchal theology and a feminist theology that places emphasis on inclusivity, diversity, and the *sensus fidelium* (dogma influenced by the voice of the congregation, not just the hierarchy).

The Curate's Egg Today

Don't ask and don't tell,
Pedophilia's the way
Priests have paved to hell.

The Curate's Egg Today is named after the phrase coined in a cartoon published in November 1895 in the British satirical magazine *Punch*. A curate is having breakfast with his bishop and is served a rotten egg. When the Bishop expresses concern the curate replies, "Oh no. my Lord, parts of it are excellent." The cartoon was titled, *True Humility* but instead it became incorporated into the English language to describe a bad situation falsely portrayed as better than it is. Note that in true English style there is room in the poem for rhyme and alliteration.

Immoral Theology

Two millennia of all-male morality
have soured sex, confessed it to death,
condemning untold souls to purgatory.
The celibate Magisterium wed power,
mating it with authority.

Forbidden impulses, fear of lust,
shame and disgust were suppressed,
hid in Pandora's box.
Theologians second guessed divine intent,
Nature, not faulty reason, was invoked.
Truth revealed in Moral Manuals,
with sex concealed in Latin text.

Immoral Theology is in hybrid form. Two unequal stanzas but with sporadic inside and end rhymes as well as alliteration and assonance. The warped Catholic theology of sexuality relates to the previous poem and the manner in which sex became an original sin and celibacy an often impossible ideal.

The pedophile crisis, perpetual misogyny, and paternalism of the Catholic Church eventually led to our departure. Archbishop Dolan sent us a Christmas card with a hand written note: "I hope you can find the perfect church; I like my church because it is a church for sinners."

I reverted to my native atheism and my wife joined the Episcopal Church, offshoot of the Church of England that I unwillingly attended in my youth.

LIFE AND LEISURE

Good Heavens!

(I can't believe it)

Why do some wives insist
There is no afterlife
Where souls will persist?
Because
If heaven did exist
Their destiny would be
Wed for eternity.

This short hybrid rhyme has two 3-line stanzas with six syllables per line. The first stanza has considerable alliteration and end rhymes that carry over to the first line of the second stanza – the rest of which relies only on satire.

Endangered Species

Primal laws dictate
species perpetuate.
When coded chromosomes
urge them to mate
they propagate.

Conceived in fervent passion,
raised with tender care,
love and lust entwined
preserve the human race.

When fate mutates
lust to distrust
and love to hate,
some children
decline to mate.

The first stanza of *Endangered Species* is rich in rhyme and alliteration, contrasting the animal manner of propagation with a shorter second stanza about humans, which is rich in emotion but devoid of poetic features. The third stanza spells the price humans may pay for lost passion in reproductive terms and reverts to rhyme. What do you think of this relationship between poetic features and content?

Heartbreak

With fractured hearts
each partner knows
love ebbs and flows
in fits and starts.

First the heart aches
under cover,
blames the other
before it breaks.

Folks don't admit,
are loath to name
oaths they defame,
sins they commit.

Sometimes its age,
and messy rows
or unkept vows
that turn the page.

Time is a thief
that robs the brain
till what remains
is loss and grief.

The stuff folks take
to soothe the soul
exerts its toll
on hearts that break.

So, in the end
they split apart:
a broken heart's
too hard to mend.

This classical poem, *Heartbreak*, tells the relatively modern tale of divorce in seven stanzas, each of four lines with only four syllables. This gives its message a terse didactic tone of inevitability. The rhyme scheme is interesting and somewhat unusual – the second and third lines and the first and last lines of each stanza have end rhymes. The second, fifth and sixth stanzas make use of alliteration.

Saint's Day Savings

Valentine's day thrift?
A man makes love to his wife
Then calls it a gift.

Saint's Day Savings is a humorous haiku after the preceding poems gloom!

Check Out

The fast lane never is.
The man in front
has lost his coupons.
The checker asks,
"endive or chicory?"
Then, "What's it cost?"
The register
runs out of change.
The bagger takes
a bathroom break.
Liquor needs someone
over twenty-one.
The next lane
is always quicker.
Its customers
are gone . . .

Checkout portrays the vicissitudes of grocery shopping in free form, also devoid of rhyme except for the last six lines (Liquor, quicker, one, gone). There are two alliterations; can you spot them?

Quit that scat!

Kids bring home to Mum
words they just heard from school chums;
Shit, piss, crap and *turds!*

Quit that scat, with an inside and an end rhyme, expresses frustration all parents know.

Cut Short

We groom and clip
whatever grows,
first the fingers
then the toes.
We call them "cures"
with Latin names,
although we know
(It's such a shame),
that only death
stops them grow.

Cut Short portrays a visit to the beauty parlor embellished with rhyme and assonance.

No Wait Loss

Watching cooking shows
switches fat to images,
swapping pounds for sounds.

This Haiku, *No Wait Loss*, has a *double entendre* title – can one lose weight this way without waiting? Its content is psycho-speculative. People who need to lose weight, or sometimes do, seem to like watching the large number of cooking shows that crowd our TV screens. It has rhyme and alliteration.

Hole in One

Those who can't play say
that golf is "a good walk spoiled."
Players stay enthralled.

This pithy Haiku, *Hole in One*, has two rhymes and an alliteration. It incorporates a well known aphorism in quotes.

AGE AND INFIRMITY

Deus ex Machina?

Once kept secret, body organs
are open to inspection:
some malignant part,
a fetus sucking thumb,
the beating heart.

Technical terms or acronyms
describe the apparatus
for each prescribed intrusion.
Echocardiogram is new for me,
my heart the part in question.

Prone on my left side,
electrodes glued to chest,
wide-eyed I view the screen
reflecting flickering images
the roving probe provides.

I see my heart pump blood,
flooding each chamber in turn.
I hear the swoosh of valves parting
like leaves in summer's breeze,
pushing life to destined places.

My able heart has kindly worked
for more than three score years and ten,
without spare parts or intervention.
Despite belief in evolution
it makes divine design debatable.

Blessed with hypertension and atrial fibrillation, my heart
rate slowed so the cardiologist was in search of structural damage

to which I was a willing witness. It was an enthralling experience. *Deus ex Machina*? is a hybrid poem; five stanzas, each of five lines with variable syllables. Stanza three is interesting – it provides an inside and end rhyme (wide-eyed, provides) as well as alliteration (prone, probe, provides) and assonance (reflecting-flickering). Stanza four has a metaphor and rhyme combined (leaves in summer breeze) and the last two lines of the final stanza echo the question raised in the poem's title as expressed in an alliteration. Even an atheist has to think twice. A lot going on!

Bonus Time

I crossed the Rubicon this year,
past three score years and ten.
Then invaded borrowed time,
stretched my allotted span
beyond the limits God allowed.

I wonder if the decrements
and ravages of age
can be viewed instead
as sacraments of living,
or testaments of thanks?

Slow stiffened gait, creaking joints,
impediments to speed,
now tend to gentler tasks,
lend themselves to strolling
in sylvan groves, minding the soul.

As one grows older, the pendulum swings between optimism & pessimism and humor & satire. *Bonus Time* reflects optimism. The three 5-line stanzas have only scattered classic traits. The first stanza combines assonance with rhyme (borrowed, allotted, allowed). The second has only a single rhyme at a distance (decrements, testaments) while the last stanza has persistent alliteration (slow, stiffened, speed, strolling, soul) that is interrupted by a single inside rhyme (tend, lend). All these blend into the background rhythm and imagery of the poem, their presence arbitrary and only noticeable *post hoc*.

Growing Old

Growing old gracefully
is oft an oxymoron.
When decrements abound
and dwindling abilities
betray life's aspirations,
then a melancholia of living
supplants a fear of dying.

A slim minority
cope with equanimity,
bearing the inevitable
in acceptance and hope,
sparing caretakers their pity.

The majority grouch and groan,
a chorus of creaking joints
or aching appendages,
which tire the caring touch,
mocking oaths to
cherish their spouse
"till death do us part."

In life's finality
senility is wedge, not bond,
driving folks asunder.
Fragile, living longer,
they wonder: What's to come?

Growing Old is decidedly on the pessimistic side and the poem is almost devoid of classical features. There are four stanzas, two of seven lines alternating with two of five lines. The syllable count is variable and there is sparse rhyme, alliteration or assonance. Only the last stanza comes alive with rhyme (finality, senility; asunder, longer, wonder) and alliteration (finality, folks, fragile). The poem clearly carries a message but would it be better as prose? What justifies a poem?

Corked

If growing older
were a flavor or odor
Men would age better.

This Haiku, *Corked,* uses the metaphor of wine as a satirical comment on men, implying they don't age as well as women. It combines assonance and rhyme (older, odor, flavor).

I'm Potent!

Nobody knew
or even suspected
what pills might do
when limp and dejected
we were re-erected.

This rhyme has a *double entendre* title, *I'm Potent,* and conveys in a single rhyming sentence an aging man's concern about virility and the benefit sought from the potency pills available today.

Going Back

I bought four years
From seven centuries or more
And thought I owned the place
Until I ventured back.

Ancient spires and stone quads,
Cloisters cool and dank,
The river flowing dark and slow,
Where daffodils adorn its banks.

Past illusions faded fast
As eclipses dim the sun;
When orbs diverge and light returns
Fresh sights and scenes emerge.

In times long gone men in mini-gowns
Paraded through the streets to lecture halls.
Now town and gown are all an urban coalition,
Blurred beyond distinction.

Today the genders share fun and space,
No longer housed like monks and nuns.
When college gates were locked at ten
Scaling rails and getting in were venial sins.

My peers did proper things, in proper ways,
Bred in Public schools, an upper crust elite,
Predictable in musts and mores.
Marching to the same beat.

Now diversity is flavor of the day,
Income, accents, skin color, class,
Sexual orientation, every perversity.
Stereotypes dissolved and swept away.

Women play rugby, men crochet,
Blazers and college tankards are *outré*,
But some traditions do persist;
Drunks and pranks still exist.

Don't call your university *Alma Mater*,
Bricks and mortar stay, but students alter;
Forget that truth and then repent,
You didn't own the place, you only rented.

44 years after I graduated from Queens' College Cambridge
in 1957, my grand- daughter Jessica graduated from Sidney Sussex
College in 2011, providing an occasion to attend Queens' College

May Ball, creating reminiscences "that make one feel so deliciously aged and sad" (George Bernard Shaw).

GoingBack blends past and present in an appropriate hybrid way that combines classical and free-form features. It has nine stanzas, each with 4 lines that have an irregular syllable count and frequent end rhymes. The second stanza has the cadence of Rupert Brooke's famous ode, *The Old Vicarage, Grantchester* (1915), evoking memories of times past in Cambridge, its river Cam, and a neighboring village.

Brighton Gardens

. . . is a white lie.
Residents know
It's not the seaside,
They're snared in wheelchairs
Trapped inside.

Dumped by
Busy kids hoping
The family wealth
Outlasts their parents'
Declining health.

Demented minds
In rooms stuffed
With antiques and odors.
Caring staff, unasked,
Mask them with scented smells.

"Never mind Dearie"
They say kindly.
In the wreckage of life
Self-esteem is a salvage operation.

A relative of ours experienced the *Brighton Gardens* kind of nursing home care that was customary into the beginning of the

21st century. In 2003 my wife became President of the retirement community we now live in, on the cusp of a nationwide change in ideology and management. Nursing homes adopted a person-first philosophy which outlawed the former kind of care that mainly met medical routines and staff convenience.

Closer to Thee

Our tower in the sky
Is where old folks do gather
Together to die.

In *Closer to Thee*, the "tower in the sky" is a luxury retirement home offering all the comforts and privileges money can buy. Included is companionship in a community of talented, like-minded folks. At the same time, we are not buffered from the reality of mortality; we are doomed to witness the suffering and dying of each of our friends in a manner that those living in their own homes and suburban communities are sheltered from.

Dwindling

In a slow footrace
between body and mind,
mobility and memory,
I ruminate: which decrement
matters most?

Bone and muscle wilt,
worn joints feel like
walking on broken glass;
This wobbly gait
is balancing on stilts.

Or is it "senior moments"
lost names dismissed,
to ease the fear of brain decay?
Either way, I can't deny
I'm dwindling away.

This pessimistic hybrid poem, *Dwindling*, has three 5-line stanzas with unequal syllable counts and only one end rhyme in each of the last two stanzas. It is mainly helped by alliteration in each stanza (Ms, Ws and Ds respectively).

AN EPIC POEM

Aids

An immigrant
it came an alien
without a name,
creeping in at the
coasts like other
cultural quirks.
Cerebrus with different
heads, it changed faces
while it spread.
In the East
it was *Kaposis sarcoma*
In the West
it was *Pneumocystis carini*
purple skin blebs
on the outside,
white webs of lung
fungus on the inside;
opportunistic organisms
that borrowed the body.

Not much was known
when it was named
*Acquired Immune
Deficiency Syndrome.*
Acquired from whom?
Whatever it was
it wasn't emancipated
liberated or even
affirmative.

Only gay men
were afflicted.

But then
the phallus is
a great inoculator.
Men are the spreaders,
inserters, intruders
of the venereal world.
Women are the vessels;
lesbians give each other
nothing (unless its love).

The lepers of Sodom
suffered slowly
eroded by organisms
their life style invited.
Cryptococcus, hepatitis,
mononucleosis,
amebiasis, herpes,
toxoplasmosis;
wasting flesh
burning fevers
bloody stools
strangled breath,
behind barriers,
behind masks,
beyond antibiotics.
Staying alive

was awful;
none did.

Scientists scurried
to find a cause
scraping frugal support
from a penny pinching
President Reagan
whose moral majority
had read *Revelations*
and recognized
Apocalypse
when they saw it.
Soon scientists
discovered gays with
AIDS differed from
those without.
More partners and
poppers, more
rimming and fisting,
more trips to
bath houses.
Evangelists and
epidemiologists agreed;
promiscuous sex was a
risk factor
What you reap depends on
how you sow the seed.
The vagina is a paved

93

passage to the ovum
but the rectum is an
absorbent entry
of fragile mucosa,
an orifice where doctors
put drugs
or force feed prisoners;
a portal where semen
seeps
into the flow of blood.

Something new was
about.
Oscar Wilde, Plato,
Michelangelo
were all immune.
Now something
invisible suppressed
the T4 cells which
assist B lymphocytes
quell infection.
Virologists,
immunologists,
venereologists,
quibbled,
vying in a quest
to find the cause.
Was it
the poppers that
open sphincters,
prolonging
orgasm?
Was it
something like
a male tampon,
leaking toxic

pathogens?
Was it
a mutant virus
embracing the
double helix like
mistletoe on oak?
Was it
an animal disease
that skipped the
biologic fence,
invading man?
Was it
antigenic overload
induced by all the
other organisms?
It was
the epidemiologists
living like Fellini
characters in gay
bars and bath houses
who ferreted
out the cause.
The clue was the cases
that came in clusters,
linked by a lone
Typhoid Mary,
spreading the disease
in silence in the baths.
In the dark no one
saw his spots.
One lonely traveling
salesman fucked
two hundred and fifty
fellow gays each year
in several years before
he sickened himself.

So, in the end,
promiscuity was
a statistical artifact.
True, viruses do
prosper at parties
but a single stoic
who goes to work
can give the common cold
to a whole factory
full of friends.

The people from Haiti
fetched migrant hopes
and non-naturalized
germs by boat.
In Miami they multiplied.
Abetted by AIDS
Toxoplasmosis gondii
grasped an opportunity
of getting to the brain.
Officials found names
for conditions buried
nameless and unknown
back home in Haiti.
Disease and discrimination
spread together.
Blacks with French
accents became tame
targets for interpreters
muffled behind masks.
Trapped between
new home prejudice
and old home persecution
sexual preference
was hardly a subject
for honest talk.

Nobody was going
to say they were gay.
Instead blame rested
on ritual or voodoo.
The inquisitors saw
reality refracted like
an object underwater.
In Haiti gay is taboo,
so married men
called massisi
do rent their bodies
to the tourist trade.
Fighting poverty they
protect their wives
from pregnancy
by anal intercourse
infecting them instead.
In Haiti AIDS
welcomed women.

Next it was needles,
proving that there was a
front door to the body.
Addicts in shooting
galleries shared syringes,
poking dull pricks
into thick veins,
breaking immune defenses
until a time when the
blameless were afflicted.
Hemophilia is a disease
of men who bleed
spread by women
on an X chromosome
that penetrates male soma
only when coupled

to an impotent Y.
To stay alive for
twenty extra years
each bleeder needs
an annual clotting
factor contribution
of two hundred
thousand donors.
Blood banks bought
blood but were not
insured against addicts
or infected gays
who sold their plasma
for quick cash to buy
another hit or fix.
The national blood
supply became
a tainted well,
a woman with a
hysterectomy,
a man after heart
surgery, were
transfused to death.

Now a ninety year old
nun and an impeccable
grandma began a new
category. "No known
risk factor" appeared.
Fear spread faster
than a virus.
Not that the virus
was slow growing.
Sponsored by
an open society
it saw its

openings.
Gays with AIDS
loved bisexuals,
Bis with AIDS
loved heterosexuals,
Bis and straights
loved their wives,
wives with AIDS
gave birth to babies.
Babies were loved by
uncles who were
junkies, aunts
who were street
walkers and mothers
who were an easy lay.
The virus multiplied
in a culture medium
of nutrient juices
a slum gullion
of sweat, saliva,
semen, blood
and colostrum
freely shared,
stirred and fermented
by love.

Hysteria and science,
illness and morals
co-mingled.
It was costly to linger.
One hundred grand
a month or more cost
for intensive care
that nobody paid.
Insurance companies
said AIDS

was self inflicted
(or had pre-existed)
Government agencies
said AIDS
was not a research
priority (nor even a
Medicaid category).
Inside intensive care
gays and junkies
lasted long enough
to go bankrupt.
Outside intensive care
landlords evicted
tenants, teachers
excluded kids,
preachers preached
damnation,
gays screeched
genocide. Then all at once
intensive care was cheap;
the innocent were infected.

It took four years
to trap and microscope,
to letter and number
the virus: HLT III.
People said
better knowing than not,
better truth than hope,
better but . . .
it was a sneaky virus
lurking inside the cell,
stalking an unsure host
leaving spoor in the
blood that could be
spotted years before

it broke cover.
People said better knowing
than not, better truth than
hope, better but . . .
an arrow or a bullet
are quicker than
a slow snare
or waiting wounded.
Instead
people said
better hope than truth,
better not than knowing
if tests suggest
you have pre-AIDS
or maybe AIDS
or maybe not.

Soon the world was
infected spread from
the hot hub of Africa
by French speaking
connections from
the old Congo to Haiti,
from Haiti to
New York when
Papa Doc died and
Port au Prince became
a paradise for gays.
Some said it was a
mutant monkey virus
evolved to man,
a second genesis,
divine revenge
for the slave trade.
Inside America
AIDS spread to every

State, became Federal
and fully emancipated.
The numbers are now
fifteen thousand
give or take a few.

Everyone is waiting
for a vaccine
in a foot race between
virus and science.
Everyone is waiting
practicing virus control by
chastity and monogamy.
Everyone is waiting
redefining old values
and discriminating.

The AIDS epidemic had its origins in the mid 1980's when I read *And the Band Played On* by San Francisco journalist Randy Shilts. A reviewer at the time described it as, "like a mystery thriller." That book is 630 pages long, which this poem condensed to about 400 lines. AIDS was published in *Psychiatric Times* in February,1968. The poem has brief irregular lines which give it a terse, urgent, didactic tone. Scattered throughout, at random, are occasional rhymes, alliteration, assonance and a few metaphors. You could test your analytic skills by applying them to one of the vertical columns seeing how many of these "classical" features you can detect. If you are tempted to read the book you might assess the degree to which the poem effectively evokes the drama and emotions of the events as they unfolded.

Epic poems have a long history dating from Greek times. They tend to highlight cultural values of national concern, of which the AIDS epidemic is an excellent example. Another of modern significance is Oliver Goldsmith's 1770 epic poem, *The Deserted Village*, which portrays an 18th century income disparity between the landed gentry and poverty stricken villagers in rural England, reminiscent of today's economic concerns (discussed in my memoir).

Like poetry in general the epic poem can employ a classical dactylic hexameter (Achilles in the *Iliad*) or free-form as in AIDS. As usual the latter can include metaphor, placement on the page, along with scattered rhyme, alliteration, and assonance.

<u>ENVOI</u>

This small volume examines 76 of the poems that I wrote from 1984 to the present between the ages of 50 and 82. A small number have been published in the lay and scientific press and almost all of them, without commentary, in my memoir, *Bits and Pieces of a Psychiatrist's Life*.

Naked Poems has a different purpose; it is a literary amateur's attempt to confront the fact that, while prose seems increasingly popular, public interest in poetry is diminishing. This volume poses and attempts to answer the questions: Why is this? What can poetry offer that prose does not?

The reader is first introduced to a variety of four traditional poetic forms expressing the same metaphor that compares words in poetry to couture in clothes. What follows is a literary analysis of each poem, establishing first its provenance before examining its form, content, and place on the page.

My hypothesis is that while prose and poetry challenge both intellect and emotion, the balance differs. Poetry may appear more opaque and it is more demanding in both arenas, with added emphasis on emotion. Opacity and emotion can be troubling and off-putting to the reader. My hope is that analysis of these poems in several different content areas will display what poetry has to offer and will increase the readers comfort and enjoyment.

Both prose and poetry are capable of a full range of content, including metaphor, imagery, humor, satire, joy, sorrow and more. But the delivery is different. Poetry is, above all, pithy; according to the Oxford English Dictionary it offers the *"essence of creativity in a vigorous and concise manner."* Perhaps the ultimate example is the Haiku which, in only seventeen syllables, conveys what may take sentences or paragraphs of prose.

To succeed, poetry employs several strategies. First, a variety of different forms in which stanzas, syllables, line breaks and placement on the page convey structure, cadence and appearance.

Second are "classical" embellishments including rhyme, alliteration or assonance combined or interacting with metaphor, imagery, creative ideas and insights.

This volume was almost finished when the *New York Times* (Sunday, August 28, 2016) published a review by David Orr of Ben Lerner's *The Hatred of Poetry*. It cast further light on Lerner's opinion that "poetry is often met with contempt rather than indifference." The reviewer notes this viewpoint "resembles any number of essays about poetry over the past hundred years, all written by poets and all making the same point with varying degrees of explicitness." Orr also finds Lerner's position "intriguing and ironic" in light of the fact that Lerner was first a poet who became more famous as a fiction writer of prose.

At the same time Orr applauds Lerner's conception that excellence in the art of poetry derives from a childlike capacity for viewing the world in creative metaphor and imagery at a time when language development is "malleable, liquid, in which anything can rise up to claim its brief purchase on the limits of our world."

I willingly concede the value of this insight but question its origins in the poetic psyche and wonder why or whether it is wise for poets to denigrate their medium in a manner that may contribute to a quarter century decline in the publics' poetry reading habits, which Orr also documents. In Shakespeare's time the audiences were largely illiterate but enamored of his talents while today a literate public increasingly rejects or ignores poetry. Poets might wonder if their muse has strayed too far away from common themes or concerns expressed in accessible forms and language.

As a psychiatrist and enthusiastic part time poet I hope this slender volume enhances the reader's joy in reading poetry and encourages a wish to continue doing so.

Clothed Again

Now our story's told;
with all its poems exposed,
the book's covers close.

ACKNOWLEDGEMENTS

Much gratitude is owed to many people.

First, posthumously, to Milwaukee Poet Jim Hazard, who, many years ago, suggested I might graduate from short stories to poetry.

To my fellow poet, sometime classmate, and friend Rick Krause, for much needed aesthetic advice and technical computer assistance in formatting and moving this oeuvre from page to press.

To my friend and mentor Tom Ban, a psychiatric polymath, for encouragement of our historical, scientific and literary collaborations over many years.

To my fellow resident, Bruce Fetter, historian and friend who listened and laughed along with me during the creation of *Naked Poems,* while bravely enduring and beating the odds of pancreatic cancer.

To those fellow residents at Saint John's who shared their wisdom and knowledge during our sessions in the Parlor, providing feedback on the final draft of *Naked Poems.*

To Mike and Nicole, staff members at Saint John's, who extricated me from the idiosyncratic clutches of my computer.

To Jessie Blackwell, graphic artist and family member, for creative cover art.

Finally, and most of all, to my "Lucy Stone" companion for forgiving any moments of emotional *in absentia* and brief lapses into despair or paranoia.

ABOUT THE AUTHOR

Barry Blackwell was born in England in 1934, spent his early childhood in India and returned home in 1943 during the Second World War to complete his education at boarding school, then Cambridge University and Guy's Hospital, and finally, the Maudsley Hospital and Institute of Psychiatry in London. He immigrated to America in 1968 at age 34 and became Chairman of Psychiatry at two medical schools with the rank of Professor in Psychiatry, Pharmacology and Behavioral Medicine.

Dr. Blackwell is an internationally known neuropsychopharmacologist with a Doctoral degree in Medicine and Pharmacology from Cambridge University, and a Master's of Philosophy degree from London University. He is a founding Fellow of the Royal College of Psychiatrists. He is author of over 250 scientific articles, book chapters and reviews, as well as author or editor of four books covering a fifty-year career with particular interests in psychosomatic medicine, psychopharmacology, medical education, and homelessness.

At age 82 he is a regular contributor of historical, biographical and controversial topics posted on the International Neuropsychopharmacology History Network website (INHN.org).

Barry's recent memoir, *Bits and Pieces of a Psychiatrist's Life* (2012), includes essays on medical and socio-political topics, short stories, poems, and anecdotes that portray his personal and professional life with humor and insight.

He is married to Kathie Eilers, a talented nurse administrator during her own successful career. Parents of four children and four grandchildren, they have lived in Milwaukee since 1980. They currently reside at an elegant retirement community on Lake Michigan where Kathie was previously President.

Barry began writing poetry in mid-career at age fifty while auditing classes at the University of Wisconsin, Milwaukee. He considers *Naked Poems* to be an amateur's attempt at encouraging others to read, enjoy, and create poetry.

Made in the USA
Monee, IL
14 October 2022